What, Me Worry?

# What, Me Worry?

## HOW TO HANG IN WHEN
## YOUR PROBLEMS STRESS YOU OUT

### Alice Fleming

**CHARLES SCRIBNER'S SONS • NEW YORK**
Maxwell Macmillan Canada • Toronto
Maxwell Macmillan International
New York • Oxford • Singapore • Sydney

Charles Scribner's Sons Books for Young Readers
Macmillan Publishing Company
866 Third Avenue, New York, NY 10022

Maxwell Macmillan Canada, Inc.
1200 Eglinton Avenue East, Suite 200
Don Mills, Ontario M3C 3N1

Macmillan Publishing Company is part of
the Maxwell Communication Group of Companies.

First edition    10  9  8  7  6  5  4  3  2  1
Printed in the United States of America

Library of Congress Cataloging-in-Publication Data
Fleming, Alice Mulcahey, date.
What, me worry? : how to hang in when your problems stress you out
/ Alice Fleming. — 1st ed.    p.    cm.
Summary: A self-help book focusing on the worries most likely to
afflict young people and on ways of overcoming them.
ISBN 0-684-19277-2
1. Worry in adolescence—Juvenile literature.
2. Teenagers—Conduct of life.
[1. Worry.    2. Conduct of life.]    I. Title.
BF724.3.W67F54  1992    152.4'6—dc20        91-31678

# CONTENTS

What, Me Worry?

# ONE

# Don't Worry, You're Not Alone

If you've ever worried about anything at all, you've got plenty of company. As a kid, Ronald Reagan worried because his family moved so often he had a hard time making friends. Carol Burnett worried because her parents were alcoholics. Novelist Graham Greene worried because he was no good at sports. Alfred Hitchcock worried because he had a stammer. Kim Basinger worried because her mom and dad didn't get along.

The truth of the matter is, everyone worries—even people who look as if they don't. Barbara Bush, for instance, and Bill Cosby, not to mention Stephen King, Michael Jordan, Meryl Streep, and Paula Abdul. What's more, they all worry about the same basic things.

What sort of things? Well, here's a list of the top five generic worries:

1. Losing someone or something you care about
2. Failing

3. Being rejected
4. Not getting something you want
5. Being embarrassed

Within these general categories, of course, there are hundreds of more specific worries that can range anywhere from extra large, like a physical handicap or a parent's illness, to extra small, like what to wear to the basketball game next week.

Worries come in an assortment of sizes and shapes, but the sensations they produce are pretty much the same. You probably don't have to be told that worrying can make you jittery and forgetful and drive you to chewing your nails, sleeping poorly, eating either too much or not enough, and acting dumber than you really are. If you're really frantic, you may develop sweaty palms, shortness of breath, a churning stomach, and a thumping sensation in your chest.

How did worry acquire such awesome powers? The answer is simple: It's triggered by one of the strongest and most primary emotions—fear. Theoretically, at least, that should be a plus. When you're in danger, you're supposed to be afraid. If you aren't, you won't do anything to protect yourself. But unfortunately, it doesn't always work that way.

Have you ever heard of people being paralyzed by fright, unable to fight back, call for help, or run away when they're being threatened? Well, worry can produce a similar, but more subtle, type of paralysis.

It's probably no accident that the word *worry* comes

from an old Anglo-Saxon word meaning "to choke." When worry gets you in its grip, it can stifle your ability to think clearly about your problems, much less try to deal with them.

In some cases, the paralysis works in a different way. Certain people—generally the calm, capable types—refuse to face up to their problems. To them, worrying is a sign of weakness or incompetence, so when they find themselves in a tight spot, they go out of their way to conceal it or, worse yet, deny that the problem exists.

If you're one of these what-me-worry? types, consider the example of General Norman Schwarzkopf. A day or two before the allied forces invaded Kuwait during the 1991 war in the Persian Gulf, a *New York Times* reporter asked the general if he was worried.

"You bet I am," snapped Schwarzkopf.

If a tough soldier like Stormin' Norman can admit to being worried, you can, too. Worrying isn't a sign that you're a dummy or a sissy; it's an appropriate reaction to a troubling situation. If you've got something on your mind, don't tell yourself you're not upset, it doesn't matter, or it will go away. Have the courage—and the wisdom—to concede that you *are* upset, it *does* matter, and—for now, at least—it *won't* go away.

Once you own up to being worried, you can stop putting so much energy into pretending you're not and direct your efforts toward coping with the problem.

There's no question that your life would be simpler—although probably quite boring—if you never had anything to worry about. But the chances of that happening are slim, so the next best thing is to get your worries under control. That means learning to take charge of them instead of letting them take charge of you.

Maybe you've heard that Bobby McFerrin song "Don't Worry, Be Happy." If only it were that easy! You can't turn off your worries with the flick of a switch or an act of the will. On the other hand, it's not that difficult either.

You may not be able to dump all your worries, but you can certainly dump some of them. You can deal with others by making them work for instead of against you, and with a little effort, you can learn to live with the rest.

# TWO

# Are You a World-Class Worrier?

Some people worry so much and so often you'd think it was their favorite sport. The classic example is Woody Allen, who gives the impression of having learned to worry before he learned to walk. David Letterman isn't much better. One of his perennial on-the-air questions is, "Have I blown the show yet?" and he isn't just kidding.

World-class worriers like Allen and Letterman have been around for ages. Back in fourteenth-century England, Geoffrey Chaucer described such people as worrying that the man would fall out of the moon. Nowadays they're more apt to worry about an asteroid plummeting to earth and destroying civilization.

It's easy to laugh at these nervous Nellies and Willy worrywarts. Some of them even laugh at themselves. But there's nothing funny about the agonies they endure. No matter how farfetched and ridiculous their worries may

5

seem to the rest of the world, they're distressingly real to them.

You may be a long way from achieving world-class status, but if your daydreams sometimes resemble nightmares and if you suspect that there's more truth than humor in Murphy's Law—which is, if anything can go wrong it will—then you could be working up to it. If so, you might be curious to know how you developed your taste for tragedy and, even more important, how you can get rid of it.

## How World-Class Worriers Get That Way

The tendency to see a catastrophe around every corner may be one of those traits, like the color of your eyes or the shape of your nose, that's inherited at birth. Researchers at the University of Oregon and the State University of New York at Purchase have studied the brain wave patterns of hundreds of subjects. In the process, they have discovered that those who exhibited more activity in the right frontal area of their brains tended to view the world as full of potential disasters, while those with greater activity in the left frontal area took a sunnier point of view.

It will be a long time before the researchers can say with certainty that brain chemistry plays a role in how much or how little people worry. In the meantime, there's no shortage of other suspects. If you come from a family of worriers, for instance, the odds are strong that you'll be one, too. You know the old saying: "You get like the people you live with."

When the American novelist Paul Bowles was growing up in the 1920s, his mother and father kept telling him that the country was a mess and would soon collapse. In 1990, the eighty-year-old Bowles expressed the same gloomy sentiments—only his predictions extended to the entire planet.

Fortunately, not even the most worry-prone families are as pessimistic as the Bowleses. But if your mom or dad, or both, are inclined to look on the dark side, it will be hard to avoid picking up on their fears.

Although family background is a key factor, you can also become a megaworrier without any help from your folks. If you've ever been bitten by a dog or stung by a bee, you've probably been wary of them ever since. Similarly, if you've ever had a painful disappointment or loss, you may be left with the feeling that the same thing, or worse, could happen again.

"Peanuts" creator Charles Schultz is an extreme example of this kind of emotional scarring. An indisputable world-class worrier, Schultz worries about crossing bridges, driving through tunnels, or traveling too far from his Santa Rosa, California, home. The cartoonist never says why (he may not know himself), but the most plausible explanation is that his mother died of cancer when he was barely out of his teens and the experience has left him feeling vulnerable to all sorts of other disasters.

\*    \*    \*

Although chronic pessimism may sound like an incurable condition, it isn't. To a large extent, worrying is a habit, and like all habits, it can be changed. If you want to cultivate a brighter outlook on life, you can begin by dropping some of the mind-sets that contribute to your negative point of view.

### • Keep your eye on the doughnut

Some years ago, a writer named McLandburgh Wilson wrote a poem that's become better known than he is:

> Twixt the optimist and pessimist
> The difference is droll:
> The optimist sees the doughnut
> But the pessimist sees the hole.

If you want to cut down on the amount of time you spend worrying, you've got to start looking at the doughnut. When you hear yourself saying (or even thinking), "Nothing ever goes right," or, "Everything happens to me," stop and ask yourself if that's really true. Surely there were times when things went well and you came out ahead. If you remember those times instead of the others, you may discover that you don't have as many reasons to worry as you think.

### • Be realistic

One of the interesting things about pessimists is that many of them are secret optimists—only their expectations are so high that nothing could possibly live up to them.

Maybe you've heard the story of the woman who consulted a psychiatrist because she was feeling depressed.

"What seems to be bothering you?" the psychiatrist asked.

"Two months ago my aunt died and left me fifty thousand dollars," the woman told him. "Then last month my cousin died and left me twenty thousand dollars."

"So what's the problem?" the psychiatrist said.

"This month"—the woman sighed morosely—"*nothing.*"

If you expect everything to work out perfectly all the time, you're not living in the real world. Be grateful for the times when things go extra well and try not to take it too hard when they don't.

### • Don't let your imagination run wild

Chronic worriers are gifted—or cursed—with vivid imaginations. Some of them get so carried away by their visions of what *could* go wrong that they never stop to think of what a slim chance there is that anything actually will. Almost anyone could be killed in a plane crash, struck by lightning, or kidnapped by terrorists, but how often do these things really happen?

A recent study by a professor at M.I.T. revealed that a person who took a domestic jet flight every single day could go, on average, more than twenty-nine thousand years before dying in a crash. The odds against similar disasters are just as strong. You hear about all sorts of horrendous catastrophes on the news, but that's because they are so unusual. If they were everyday events, they wouldn't be news.

## • Remember that feelings aren't facts

Just because you're afraid something will happen doesn't mean that it will. Charles Schulz gets anxious at the thought of traveling, but the few times he's tried it, he's come home safe and sound. Carol Burnett used to think that people wouldn't like her if she didn't agree with everything they said. When she got up the nerve to express her own opinions, however, she discovered that nobody minded in the least.

Some of your own worries may not reflect the true picture. Your friends may not see your strict curfew as a sign that your parents are weird. And even though you think your body is misshapen, it may look fine to everyone else.

If you worry about letting your parents down by not excelling at sports or making the honor roll every term, consider the possibility that their expectations may not be as high as you imagine. Instead of living in fear of not always being first or best, concentrate on doing as well as you can. Your performance may improve when you're not so uptight. If it doesn't, your parents will survive.

## *The Snowball Effect*

The Irish have an expression for worrying about imaginary problems. They call it "knocking your shins against a stool that isn't there." That's okay for ordinary worriers, but if you're going for the gold, you won't settle for one stool that isn't there. You'll insist on bumping into whole stacks of them. The bottom one is your original worry. The rest are all the other worries you pile on top of it.

Let's say you're home alone and it's getting dark. You suddenly begin to wonder if the back door is locked. If it isn't, someone could get into the house and kill you. You can see yourself trying to hide, but the gunman—or maybe it's an ax murderer—searches the house and finds you. The rest is too horrible to think about. But by this time you're too petrified to think anyway.

If you calmed down and backtracked a few steps, however, you'd quickly realize that you weren't really sure whether the back door was unlocked in the first place, much less whether there was a murderer outside waiting to claim you as his latest victim.

*Catastrophizing* is the official name for the habit of letting small worries snowball into large ones. The best cure for it is to distract yourself by getting involved in something else—a TV show or a good book, for instance. It's a proven fact that the human mind can't think of two things at the same time. The minute you turn your thoughts in a different direction, your worries will disappear.

It's probably expecting too much to suggest that you laugh at your own catastrophizing, but you might try memorizing the following verse, which an anonymous poet dedicated to those who always fear the worst:

> Suppose one thing,
> Suppose another,
> Suppose your mother
> Was a bullfrog's brother.

Recite it to yourself the next time your worries start to snowball. It might keep them from developing into an avalanche.


## How to Get off the Worry-go-round

One of the cures for excessive worrying—and the one that is most often prescribed by mental health experts—is to set aside some time each day to do nothing but worry. Twenty minutes is the recommended amount. Psychologist Wayne Dyer suggests dividing the time into two segments—ten minutes in the morning and another ten in the afternoon. You can set your own schedule. Just don't select the period before bedtime or you'll have a hard time getting to sleep. When you find yourself worrying at other times, stop and save it for your worry break.

As time goes on, you'll find that you don't need as much worry time as you used to. Eventually, you may not need any at all. For reasons psychologists can't completely explain, deliberate worrying seems to decrease the need to worry. Perhaps it's like eating too many peanuts and never wanting to look at them again. Still another possibility is that worrying loses its appeal when it can't divert you from more productive pursuits.

The worry experts also suggest keeping track of your

worries by writing them down in a diary or journal. This will relieve you of the burden of carrying them around in your head and will also make them seem more manageable. Instead of coming at you from every direction at unexpected moments, they'll be right there in one place where you can fret over them whenever you want to.

Once every few weeks or so, go back and read over your list. You may be surprised to see that some of the things you worried about didn't happen, that others weren't as bad as you expected, and that still others turned out fine. Whatever happened, it should be quite clear that worrying—world class or otherwise—didn't have the slightest effect on the outcome.

# THREE

# What's Done Is Done

Unless you're specially blessed or enormously lucky, there's at least one thing in your past that you wish hadn't happened. Maybe you didn't get what you wanted for your birthday, or your best friend moved to Atlanta, or your mom and dad got divorced. Maybe it was something even worse.

Whatever it was, you may find yourself going over the incident again and again, brooding about how unfair it was, and imagining how much happier you'd be if things had gone the other way. If so, it's about time you stopped. What happened in the past is history and all the worrying in the world won't change it.

That doesn't mean you have to be a Pollyanna, the heroine of Eleanor H. Porter's 1913 novel who could find a ray of sunshine in the worst calamity. You're entitled to feel angry, sad, discouraged, defeated, or even heart-

14

broken when something goes wrong in your life. But not forever.

In the course of her long career in radio and television, TV personality Sally Jessy Raphael has been fired no less than eighteen times. Each time she gave herself three days to stay home and feel sorry for herself. Then she started mapping out a campaign for finding another job.

It must have taken Sally Jessy Raphael a lot longer than three days to recover from her disappointment. Very few hurts heal that quickly. But she was smart enough to realize that there was nothing she could do to change the situation, so she might as well put it behind her and get on with her life.

That's really all you *can* do when these kinds of setbacks occur; but recognizing that fact is one thing, acting on it is something else.

In 1983, a relatively unknown actor named Kevin Costner gave up the lead in one film to take a smaller but meatier part in *The Big Chill*. Two weeks before the picture's release, the director decided that it would be more effective to have the character Costner played talked about rather than be seen. Costner's scenes wound up on the cutting room floor and his nonappearance immediately became one of Hollywood's inside jokes.

Another actor might have reacted to this turn of events by drowning his disappointment in alcohol, obliterating it with drugs, or developing a lifelong grudge against the director. Not Costner.

"I was in a very good movie called *The Big Chill* and was cut out of it," he said later. "It didn't destroy me the way people thought it should because I had a bigger sense of myself than that one movie."

Having a bigger sense of yourself is the key to surviving even the cruelest disappointments. In 1921, Franklin D. Roosevelt was stricken with polio and left crippled in both legs. He could have spent the rest of his life bemoaning the end of his promising political career. Instead he returned to his law practice and evenually to politics.

You can bet there were moments when Franklin D. Roosevelt raged against his handicap. You can bet he had tearful memories of the days when he could walk without leg braces and crutches. You can bet he asked, "Why me?" a million times. And yet Roosevelt never succumbed to self-pity and refused to accept pity from anyone else.

"No sob stuff," he would tell his family and friends whenever they threatened to get mushy.

Roosevelt's biographers are almost unanimous in their opinion that his illness made him a wiser and more dedicated leader and increased his sympathy for the poor and afflicted. Instead of leaving him a broken man, his handicap enabled him to develop precisely the qualities he needed to become one of the country's most admired presidents.

One of the strongest arguments against worrying about the past is that it can keep you from doing your best in the present. In the mid-1920s, Walt Disney produced a series of movie cartoons starring a character called Oswald Rabbit.

The series was so successful that Disney made a trip to New York to ask the man who distributed the cartoons to give him a raise. The distributor not only said no, he suggested that Disney lower his price. If he didn't, the distributor, who already owned the rights to Oswald Rabbit, was planning to produce it on his own.

Walt Disney refused to back down and stalked out of the distributor's office in a rage. He could have spent the entire three-day train trip back to Los Angeles worrying about how he had been muscled out of his only profitable cartoon character. Instead he got out his sketch pad and pencils and set to work. By the time the train reached California, Oswald's replacement had been born. He was a mouse with a round head and ears, pipestem legs, white gloves, and a pair of oversized shoes. Disney named him Mickey.

The Chinese ideogram for *crisis* is a combination of two other characters. One stands for *danger* and the other for *opportunity*. Opportunities appear in many forms. Although you can't count on a crisis to turn you into a better or more successful person, if you can weather it without becoming angry or bitter, or spending the rest of your life feeling sorry for yourself, you'll unquestionably come out a stronger one.

Perhaps the only instance in which worrying about the past isn't useless is when you've done something that wasn't right. In that case, the uneasy feeling you get every time you think about it is only one part worry. The rest is guilt.

You can't undo an act that was wrong or hurtful to somebody else, but you can relieve your guilt by trying to make amends. You can repay a storekeeper for items you've stolen, for example. If you're too embarrassed to do it in person, do it by mail. You don't have to sign your name.

By the same token, you can apologize to someone you've hurt. Apologies aren't easy, but think of how much better you'll feel when you get the incident off your chest. If you're too chicken to deal with a face-to-face apology, send a card or a note. In most cases, all you have to say is "I'm sorry."

If the episode occurred some time ago and you're no longer in touch with the person involved, or if bringing it up at this late date would involve too many explanations and complications, you can satisfy your conscience in other ways. Try doing a special kindness for somebody else, donating part of your allowance to a worthy cause, or performing some type of community service.

Still another option is simply to forgive yourself and resolve to be more careful in the future. Everyone makes mistakes now and then. Why should you be any different?

# FOUR

# What Will Be Will Be

If there's anything more futile than worrying about the past, it's worrying about the future. Unless you're a certified seer or prophet—and who is?—you have no way of knowing what the future holds. Most of the time it isn't what you expect. Half the time it doesn't even come close.

In 1969 a minor British official confidently predicted, "No woman in my time will be prime minister." A decade later, the official—Margaret Thatcher—was elected to the post.

Ten minutes can bring as many surprises as ten years. The fans who trooped into Candlestick Park in San Francisco for the third game of the 1989 World Series had no idea they were going to witness an earthquake instead of a ball game.

Considering how often the unexpected happens, it doesn't make sense to get hung up on problems that

19

may—or may not—occur in a few weeks, months, or years. But some people do it anyway. If you happen to be one of them, take a cold, hard look at the situation that's bugging you and ask yourself two questions:

1. Are you sure it's going to happen?
2. Will worrying about it do any good?

When the English ballerina Dame Margot Fonteyn was preparing for her New York debut in 1949, she spent almost as much time worrying as she did rehearsing. "I felt absolutely certain that I was not the kind of dancer New York was going to like," she wrote in her autobiography. "I was very frightened."

Dame Margot's rehearsal time paid off, but her worrying time was a total loss. New York audiences and critics loved her, and her American debut made her an international star.

Even if the problems you anticipate *do* happen, who's to say they'll be as dreadful then as they seem right now? Worries can be like summer storms—full of thunder and dark clouds in the distance but only a few sprinkles when they finally arrive.

If you're dubious, think of some of the things you worried about in the past. When you were in kindergarten, you probably wondered how you'd ever survive first grade. It was scary to think of learning to read and write and spending the entire day in school. Then when you got to first grade, you discovered that it wasn't such a big deal after all.

20

You'll have similar experiences at every stage of your life. When you're in grade school, high school looks hard. In high school, it's college, and in college, it's going out and finding a job.

President Harry S. Truman used to tell a story that shows how time can change your perspective. When Truman was first elected to the Senate, an older and more experienced politician took him aside and told him not to be intimidated by his new job.

"For the first six months you'll wonder how you got here," the man said. "After that, you'll wonder how the rest of them got here."

One of the dangers of worrying about problems before they happen is that your fears could turn out to be self-fulfilling prophecies. In case you're not familiar with the term, *self-fulfilling prophecy* means that when you believe something will turn out badly, you're less inclined to try to stop it, thereby increasing the chances that it will.

A few years ago, a team of psychologists conducted an experiment in which they asked a group of subjects to compete in a test of leg strength against people they didn't know. Half the subjects were told that their opponents were varsity track stars, while the other half were told that their opponents were people with leg injuries. In almost every instance, the subjects who thought their rivals were well-trained athletes did poorly, and those who thought their opponents were injured did well.

You can create your own self-fulfilling prophecies by being so convinced you'll never make the soccer team or learn to play chess that you won't even take the first steps. If you stopped programming yourself to fail, you might discover that you're quite capable of doing well.

Trying to peer too far into the future is a chancy business because the farther ahead you look, the less you're likely to see. What seems like a sure thing right now may seem wildly ridiculous a few years from now. The situation may change. You may change. Something else may intervene.

When Michael J. Fox was in grade school, he dreamed of playing hockey for the Toronto Maple Leafs. He would have been devastated if anyone had told him then that he didn't stand a chance. But by the time he reached high school and realized that he was never going to be tall enough to become a professional athlete, he no longer cared. By then he was playing the guitar in a rock band and had his sights set on a career in music. But as everyone knows, that didn't work out either.

Worrying about the future of the country or the world is even more pointless than worrying about your own future. It's important to be interested in, and work for, causes you believe in, but don't lose your perspective. The fact that you're concerned won't automatically change the course of history.

You can stew all you want about nuclear weapons, the environment, or poverty, but worrying won't produce world peace, clean air, or full employment. If you want to make an impact, you have to be a doer, not a stewer. That means getting involved by working with other concerned citizens to raise public awareness of these problems and to push for the adoption of laws aimed at solving them.

Sensible people don't ignore the future, but they don't live in it to such an extent that they can't do anything in the present. They also know the difference between worrying about the future and planning for it.

San Francisco 49ers quarterback Joe Montana never knows precisely what his team will be up against on the football field, but he'd rather be prepared than be surprised. Montana spends the week before every game memorizing game plans, studying film clips, and analyzing his opponents' defenses—a tactic that usually pays off with a win for the 49ers.

Unless the world comes to an end—which it never seems to—you know that some things are bound to happen. Assignments will come due. Your allowance will run out. Summer vacation will end.

If there's something you can do to prepare for the predictable events in your life, by all means do it. If there isn't, follow the example of Albert Einstein. "I never think of the future," he said. "It comes soon enough."

# FIVE

## Occasional Worries

Some situations are surefire worry producers. The most obvious ones include taking a test, performing in public, competing in a sports event, and undergoing a medical or dental procedure.

Fortunately, none of these are everyday occurrences. If they were, they might not bother you so much—although there's no guarantee. The world famous cellist Pablo Casals complained of lifelong stage fright, and after more than thirty years in television, weatherman Willard Scott, Jr., still lives in fear of making a fool of himself on the air.

Few performers are that apprehensive, but all of them are subject to—and actually welcome—a few twinges of anxiety. If anything, they worry when they're *not* worried. "If I don't feel tense," says Liza Minnelli, "I know I'm not revved up to do my best."

People who aren't in show business sometimes feel the

same way. Not long ago, a team of psychologists at the University of Michigan conducted an experiment in which they took two groups of college students, presented them with a puzzlelike task, and asked them to predict how well they would do. The first time around, the students who thought they'd do poorly performed as ably as those who thought they'd do well.

The researchers then presented the two groups with a second test, only this time they gave them a pep talk in which they assured the students that they were all very bright and capable and had nothing to worry about. The pep talk had no effect on the students who already expected to do well, but it seemed to mar the performances of those who didn't.

The researchers concluded that the latter group had their own strategy for coping with difficult tasks. It consisted of expecting the worst and working hard to avoid it, a trick they apparently needed to play on themselves in order to do well.

Obviously, a limited amount of worry is normal, even desirable, when you're under pressure. But if your worries go beyond the acceptable limit and leave you panicked to the point of being barely able to function, you've got to take steps to control them. Here are three ways to do that:

## 1. Know what to expect

Fear of the unknown is a major ingredient in occasional worries. That's why it's helpful to find out as much as you can about a situation in advance. If you're nervous about undergoing a medical procedure, for instance, ask your doctor what it involves, how long it will take, and whether you'll be given anything to relieve the pain.

It goes without saying that you should prepare for a test with lots of studying, but you might also ask the teacher what material will be covered, what's especially important, and whether the questions will be essay or multiple choice. If you're going to appear on a stage or in an athletic facility where you've never performed, try to see it in advance so you can familiarize yourself with the setting. Getting the feel of the place will help cut down on your nervousness.

When you're faced with an unfamiliar social situation—a formal party or dance or a dress-up dinner, for instance—do your best to find out what's going to happen and when, who's going to be there, and if there's anything special you should do, wear, or bring. If you can reduce your chances of being thrown by the unexpected, you'll have one less thing to worry about.

## 2. Give yourself mental rehearsals

One of the best ways to ease performance-related anxieties—that is, the uneasiness you feel about such things as competing in a track meet, participating in a spelling bee, or standing up to give a book report—is to give yourself mental rehearsals. Visualize what you're going to do, step by step, and imagine yourself doing it exactly right.

If you rehearse your performance several times before the actual event, you'll not only become more accustomed to doing it the way you want, you'll also be able to spot and correct glitches before they happen. Gymnast Mary Lou Retton, who won a gold medal at the 1984 Olympics, included this kind of visualization in her bedtime routine.

"Before I dropped off to sleep inside the Olympic Village," she recalls, "I did what I always do before a major competition—mindscripted it completely. I mentally ran through each routine, every move, imagining everything done perfectly."

Mental rehearsals aren't a substitute for action. You still have to know what you're doing and practice doing it well. But going over your moves in advance will increase your self-confidence and keep your natural abilities from being impaired by your anxieties.

### 3. Breathe easy

Many of the physical symptoms of worry—dizziness, shortness of breath, chest pains, nausea, and the shakes— can be worries all by themselves.

You have these symptoms because when you're frightened, your adrenal gland secretes a special hormone that increases your heartbeat, speeds up your breathing, and tenses the muscles in your arms and legs. This would be a decided advantage if you had to react in a real emergency, such as dashing out of a burning building or fleeing from a grizzly bear, but when the emergency has been generated by your own anxieties, your tension has no place to go. Happily, there's a simple exercise you can perform to get rid of it.

Start by sitting in a relaxed position with your hands

in your lap and your feet flat on the floor. Then take a deep breath and fill your lungs with air. Hold it for three full seconds. (You can measure them by counting to yourself, "One thousand one. One thousand two. One thousand three.") Exhale very slowly, and as you do, relax your muscles and think of something pleasant—a field of daisies, for instance, or a sky full of twinkling stars. Remain in this relaxed position for a minute or two. If you still feel anxious, try it again.

Occasional worries have a bad habit of looming so large in your mind that they block out everything else. You'll have to make a special effort to cut them down to size. No matter how harrowing the ordeal you're facing, try to remember that it won't last forever. In an hour or so, possibly less, it will be all over and your life will get back to normal. If you can imagine how much better you'll feel then, the thought will have a tranquilizing effect and you'll start to feel better right away.

# SIX

# Decisions, Decisions

Even if you don't come close to being a world-class worrier, you must have noticed that your worry meter goes up a few degrees—maybe more—when you have to make a decision. It happens to everyone and for understandable reasons: They—and you—are afraid of making the wrong choice.

Every decision is a gamble. There's always the risk that you won't be completely happy with the way things turn out, and the even bigger risk that you'll be completely miserable. Still, there's no way you can get through life without ever making up your mind about anything. Some people try it. They either go along with the crowd or rely on other people for advice.

The downside to that approach is that if everything works out okay, they can't take any credit for it. If things don't work out, they have to take the blame. In either case, they're letting other people do their thinking. What the permanently undecideds don't seem to realize is that *not* making a choice is a choice too, and it's seldom a very good one.

Since you can't avoid making decisions, you might as well learn to make them intelligently. This will not only cut down on the amount of worrying that goes into making them, it will increase your chances of being satisfied with the results.

## *Small* d *Decisions*

There are decisions and there are Decisions. The small *d* kind are the ones you make all the time—what to wear, which video to rent, what kind of pizza to order. Some of them can be a real pain. As the American humorist Josh Billings pointed out, "It is the little bits of things that fret and worry us; we can dodge an elephant, but we can't dodge a fly."

Instead of driving yourself batty trying to make up your mind about trivial matters, try to remember that whatever you decide, it's not going to affect the course of your life in any significant way or, more likely, in any way at all.

Unless your outfit is either an absolute knockout or an absolute mess, very few people will notice, or care, what you're wearing. If you don't like the video you selected, you can look for a better one the next time around. As for the pizza, it's not the only slice you're ever going to eat, so does it really matter whether you order pepperoni or plain?

If you regularly spend more time than you should on small *d* decisions, stop flip-flopping and make up your mind, even if you have to toss a coin or say eenie, meenie, minie, mo. Life is too short to worry about trifles.

## *Big* D *Decisions*

Big *D* decisions require more serious thought and usually take longer to reach—and so they should. You may have heard of famous men and women who made up their minds to do something and never once faltered in their resolve, but if you study their lives more closely, you'll see that most of them were plagued by doubts.

Abraham Lincoln spent months weighing the pros and cons of issuing the Emancipation Proclamation. Sir Thomas More took even longer to oppose King Henry VIII's defiance of the Pope. He knew that the wrong decision would cost him his head.

Your own big *D* decisions may be less momentous, but they deserve careful reflection just the same. Maybe you're thinking of giving up your music lessons because people tease you about playing the flute; or you're trying to get up the nerve to tell your mom how much you dislike the current man in her life; or you're torn between taking French, which you'd like to learn, or Spanish, which all your friends are taking.

The American author and publisher Elbert Hubbard knew what he was talking about when he said, "It does not take much strength to do things, but it requires great strength to decide on what to do."

It's difficult to sort through the different, usually con-flicting, emotions big *D* decisions create. What strikes you as the right move one minute may strike you as the wrong move the next. You may be annoyed to find yourself in a stall and even more annoyed because you can't get out of it. To add to your worries, there's the nagging suspicion that you'll discover you made the wrong decision when it's too late to back out.

Instead of agonizing over your choices, there are a num-ber of tactics you can use to get over the emotional hurdles and reach a decision.

## 1. Imitate Ben Franklin

One of the chief problems involved in making decisions is that it's impossible to keep all the reasons for making one choice rather than another in your head at the same time.

Benjamin Franklin solved this dilemma with a system he called moral or prudential algebra. He recommended taking a sheet of paper and dividing it into two col-umns. List all the reasons for on one side and all the reasons against on the other. Keep the list around for a few days so you can add to it as other thoughts occur to you.

When you can't think of any more reasons, compare the two columns to see which one contains the stronger arguments. Occasionally, they'll balance each other out and you'll have to follow your instincts, but most of the time you'll get an accurate reading on what you ought to do.

## 2. Anticipate the worst

You can relieve at least some of the tension that goes with decision making by asking yourself (a) what's the worst thing that can happen as a result of my choice? and (b) can I accept it?

Charles A. Lindbergh never minimized the dangers he faced when he embarked on his famous solo flight from New York to Paris in 1927. When someone asked him why he was taking along only a few sandwiches and some water, the twenty-five-year-old mail pilot replied bluntly, "If I get to Paris, I won't need any more, and if I don't, I won't need any more either."

Few decisions are a matter of life and death, but many of them can result in serious disappointments. If you try out for cheerleader, you may not make it. If you invite someone special to your Halloween party, he or she might say no. If you set your sights on an Ivy League college, you could be rejected. Consider these possibilities before you proceed. Knowing you can live with your choices, however poorly they turn out, will make it easier to decide what to do.

## 3. Have a backup plan

Your decision will be less hair-raising if you create a safety net for yourself by thinking of what your options will be if things don't go according to plan.

When Anjelica Huston was sixteen years old, her father, film director John Huston, took her out of school to star in a movie he was making called *A Walk with Love and*

*Death*. It was an irresistible opportunity, but it was also a serious risk. Anjelica had never taken an acting class and she didn't want to ruin her career before it even got started.

"If I'm a deadly flop," she kept telling herself, "there's still time for me to start all over again."

The thought sustained her during the filming, but her worries proved to be well founded; both she and the film got panned. Because she had already prepared herself for this possibility, Anjelica wasn't completely shattered by the experience, and following her backup plan, she did indeed start a whole new film career later on.

## 4. Do your homework

When you have to make a decision—especially if it's one that will require an investment of time, effort, or money—it's wise to do some homework. If you get the facts, your choice will be based on solid information, not guesswork. Moreover, as you learn more about the subject, you may automatically eliminate a few of your options and thus narrow the field you have to choose from. By the time you're finished, your decision may be already made.

Comparison shopping for athletic shoes, for example, may turn up only one style that feels comfortable and is in your price range. Sending for brochures about computer camps may lead you to decide that you're not that interested after all.

Informed decisions stand the best chance of working out well, so before you make up your mind about any important matter, take the time to read up on the subject or talk to someone who's in a position to provide some useful advice.

## *Right and Wrong*

Among the hardest decisions to make are the ones that require moral courage—standing up for what's right, for instance, or blowing the whistle on some type of wrongdoing. Unless there's a pressing need to act, it's easier, and less risky, not to get involved.

A few years ago a junior researcher at Tufts University suggested that her superior might have faked the findings in an important scientific paper. The researcher, Dr. Margot O'Toole, was dismissed from her job. Exiled by the scientific community, she was reduced to answering the phones at her brother's moving company.

It was four years before O'Toole was able to find another research job and five years before investigators at the National Institute of Health in Washington finally concluded that she had been right all along.

At this stage in your life, your opportunities to display moral courage will probably be more limited. It may be a question of deciding whether to report the kid you saw stealing things from another kid's locker or whether to violate your crowd's unwritten law and invite the class outcast to sit with you at lunch.

If you don't have a strict conscience like Margot O'Toole's, or if you're not the type to stick your neck out or your nose in, you'll probably have trouble deciding what to do. In wrestling with the decision, remember that even if you create problems for yourself, you can never go wrong by doing the right thing.

In cases where the decision involves some type of wrongdoing on your part, there are other factors to consider. Drinking, speeding, driving without a license, or experimenting with sex or drugs could cause you physical harm. Many of these activities, along with such other offenses as stealing or vandalizing property, are also against the law.

During his tenure in the 1950s as one of New York City's most popular mayors, Robert F. Wagner, Jr., had a motto, "If in doubt, don't." Remember that the next time you're tempted to take a chance on doing something that could get you into serious trouble. Even if you get away with it, you may be letting yourself in for a guilt trip, not to mention all the worries you'll have wondering if you might get caught.

You probably know all too well that not every decision works out for the best. It's not necessarily because of your poor judgment. There may be problems you didn't foresee or factors you couldn't control. These things happen, but with any luck you may be able to learn from your mistakes.

Some years ago, Victor Kiam, who later became a multimillionaire through his marketing of Remington shavers, let his advisers talk him out of obtaining the rights to a new product called Velcro that turned out to be a runaway success.

"I could get upset about that," says Kiam, "but I look

at it as just another blip on the road. Besides, if I hadn't learned from that lapse of judgment—by having more confidence in my advisers than I did in myself—I never would have gone on to buy Remington."

Few mistakes lead to such happy endings, but if you did what seemed best at the time, don't blame yourself. Instead of constantly rehashing the situation and trying to figure out what you did wrong, chalk it up to experience and give yourself credit for trying.

As President Theodore Roosevelt once remarked, "The only man who never makes a mistake is the man who never does anything."

# SEVEN

## Looking Good

If there's one habit that's epidemic among kids around the ages of twelve or thirteen, it's worrying about their looks. Up until now, you may not have paid much attention to the size of your ears or the slant of your chin, but with the onset of adolescence, these and other aspects of your appearance are likely to become major concerns.

For the next couple of years, you'll probably be spending a lot of time in front of your mirror scrutinizing yourself from every angle and cataloging your various flaws. Your mouth has the wrong shape, your hair is hopeless, your feet are too big, you're in danger of developing terminal acne.

Although you probably don't want to think of yourself as "going through a stage," that's the main explanation for this sudden fixation on your appearance. You're slowly but surely developing into an adult and, for perhaps the first time in your life, you're becoming seriously aware of your body. Unfortunately, this also happens to be the time when your body isn't at its best.

It seems grossly unfair that this transition has to occur at precisely the age when looking good is your passport to social acceptance and your worst nightmare is having some physical defect that might set you apart from your peers or put you in line for teasing or rejection. But fair or not, that's the way it is.

It's going to take you a few years to get through this stage, but to make sure you don't talk yourself into an inferiority complex while you're waiting, you have to understand a few facts about adolescent development. When you know what's going on, you'll realize that you and your problems aren't so freaky after all.

## Height

Most boys start to grow taller around the age of fourteen, but the process that's known as the adolescent growth spurt can begin almost anytime between the ages of ten and a half and sixteen. Girls tend to shoot up earlier. Twelve is the average age, but anytime between nine and a half and fourteen and a half is considered normal.

The growth spurt lasts for approximately two years. During that time, you may add as much as eight inches to your height. You'll continue to grow, but at a much slower rate, until somewhere around your eighteenth birthday. A few people gain another inch—although rarely much more—before the process officially ends at the age of twenty-one.

Since girls generally start their growth spurts earlier than boys, if you're a girl, you may worry about towering over some of the boys you know. Conversely, if you're a boy, you may worry about feeling like a midget next to some of the girls. In most cases, the boys soon catch up and things even themselves out.

If they don't, there isn't much you can do about it. If you're a girl, however, you can be thankful that being on the tall side is no longer the handicap it was back in the Victorian era, when delicate, doll-like women were all the rage. Nowadays, a few extra inches is perfectly acceptable, and for sports-minded girls, it can actually be a plus.

Boys generally find it harder to accept being short. It can bar them from team sports and leave them vulnerable to such nicknames as Shrimp and Shorty. Still, that's about the worst that can happen, and although it might be a nuisance, it hardly seems unbearable. Certainly, short stature has never been an obstacle to male achievement. The Nobel Prize-winning economist Milton Friedman is five feet four inches tall. So is the 1991 Masters golf champion, Ian Woosnam. And believe it or not, there's a basketball guard—Muggsy Bogues of the Charlotte Hornets—who's five feet three.

## Weight

There aren't many kids (or adults either, for that matter) who are satisfied with their weight. The majority of them worry about being too fat or about having the fat in all

Looking Good

the wrong places, but a fair number—usually boys—
worry about looking like stick figures.

You'd never know it to look at him now, but actor
John Goodman used to be one of those skinny guys. Then
somewhere in midadolescence he started to get chunky,
and the next thing you know, he was a two-hundred-
pound muscle man and the starting offensive and defen-
sive lineman on his high school football team.

Admittedly, Goodman's pattern was unusual, but thin
boys usually fill out to some degree as they get into their
teens, and the ones who aren't so thin tend to develop
muscles where they used to have fat.

Many girls put on a few pounds prior to the onset of
menstruation and then gradually lose them in their mid-
or late teens. There's hope for the bony types, too. The
majority look much less scrawny when their breasts develop and their hips acquire a more definite shape.

What all this means is that the tendency to be either
plump or lean may be just one more symptom of that
stage you're going through. If you'll only be patient, your
weight problems will solve themselves.

If you're not patient, or if your weight problems seem
more than just temporary, you may want to launch a
campaign to increase or decrease the numbers that keep
showing up on your scale. Obviously, the easiest way to
gain weight is to eat more. Help yourself to larger portions
at mealtime and feel free to snack in between. Stay away
from candy and cakes, however, and stick with foods that
can offer you more nourishment, such as milk, nuts, gra-
nola, crackers, and peanut butter.

Make sure, too, that you don't go into a feeding frenzy just before mealtime. Snack at least two hours prior to lunch or dinner so you won't spoil your appetite. If you don't have much of an appetite to begin with, try getting more fresh air and exercise. The combination is a fool-proof formula for producing hunger pangs.

If your goal is to lose weight, don't try to do it with miracle pills, potions, and programs. Some of them are dangerous, many don't work, and virtually none are recommended for young people. If you want to shed a few pounds, do it the no-frills way. Drink skim instead of regular milk (but make sure it's fortified with vitamins A and D) and cut down on high-calorie items like desserts, candy, second helpings, and between-meal snacks. If you feel deprived without something to munch on, prepare a batch of celery and carrot sticks and leave them in the refrigerator. Be sure to put them near the front so they'll be the first thing you spot when you make your raid.

If you're hoping to lose more than five or six pounds or have a chronic illness or health problem, don't embark on any kind of diet without consulting your doctor.

## Skin

Zits are not only one of the worst plagues of adolescence, they have a maddening habit of showing up just when you want to look your best. The timing is strictly coincidental, but there's a biological explanation for your complexion problems. Because of the hormonal changes that take place during puberty, the oil glands in your face are working overtime. The excess oil they secrete frequently pushes its way to the surface of the skin and forms pimples and blackheads.

One cure that is not recommended is vigorous scrubbing several times a day. It won't clear up a bad complexion and it could cause your skin to become irritated. Picking at and squeezing your pimples isn't the answer either. If you break the skin, the spot will only become more obvious.

The best approach is to apply one of the over-the-counter lotions or creams that are recommended for teenage skin problems. If your pimples are too numerous to count, ask your doctor to refer you to a skin specialist. Dermatologists, as they are called, have special techniques for clearing up even the most persistent cases of acne.

If a particularly unsightly pimple appears when you're going someplace special, you can disguise the redness and swelling with one of those cover sticks designed to conceal scars and dark circles under the eyes. But don't use it on a regular basis. Most makeup contains oils, which will only aggravate your skin problems.

When you're fretting over your latest skin eruption, it helps to avoid inspecting it at close range. Stand farther back from the mirror, or better still, look in one that's full-length. When you do, you'll see that the blemish is all but eclipsed by your hair, your eyes, your clothes, and your smile. Most people will see you from this distance rather than up close. That means only the ones with the sharpest eyes will notice your complexion, but even if they do, so what? They've had their share of pimples, too.

## Ears, Noses, and Chins

You may think that your ears stick out, your chin recedes, or your nose is ridiculously large. You could be right, but before you get too depressed, you should realize that your problems may not be permanent.

At this age, your face is still getting its act together. Your ears reached 85 to 90 percent of their adult size by the time you were five or six years old, but your head may be slow in catching up to them. In addition, the chin you have now may not be the one you end up with. Chins don't mature until the age of eighteen in girls and twenty-one in boys.

Noses reach their adult size around the age of thirteen in girls and fifteen in boys, but again, what you see isn't necessarily what you get. Your face will eventually develop adult proportions, and a nose that looks out of place on a teenager may be quite distinguished on an adult. Look at Barbra Streisand.

If you're not convinced, plastic surgery may be an option, provided your parents agree and you're willing to put up with the pain, bruising, and swelling. Plastic surgeons can also remodel ears, chins, and assorted other body parts.

While it's comforting to know that surgical help is available, it's rarely necessary to do anything that drastic.

As you get older and develop more self-confidence, you'll probably feel more comfortable with the looks you were born with. You may also discover that you have several good features. If you hadn't been so busy worrying about the bad ones, you would have noticed them a long time ago.

If you're determined to find something wrong with your appearance, you'll never have to worry about failing. There aren't many perfect tens in this world, and the few who make it usually get an extra boost from makeup artists, hair stylists, and fashion designers. While there's no law against fretting about your freckles, birthmarks, braces, or glasses, don't forget that they look ten times worse to you than they do to anyone else.

Dartmouth College psychologist Dr. Robert Cleck has conducted an experiment that demonstrates this point. His research team used makeup to simulate a facial scar on a group of subjects who were about to be introduced to a stranger. Unbeknownst to the subjects, the marks were removed before the introductions took place, and yet in every case, the subjects reported feeling uncomfortable because the stranger had stared at their scars.

Instead of worrying about the aspects of your appearance that are beyond your control, why not concentrate on the areas where improvement is a real possibility? Something as simple as changing your hairstyle, for instance, could give you a whole new image.

You might also give some thought to the type of clothes you've been wearing. Styles that look great on some body types don't do anything at all for others. It's nice to be up on the latest fashions, but don't do it at the risk of not looking your best.

If you have special problems such as being unusually short or tall or having extra large hips, choose styles that play them down. Your local library probably has a book or two that can offer more specific advice. You can also find tips in some of the magazines.

Boys as well as girls should study the shades that complement their particular hair color and skin tones. Wearing the wrong colors can make you look drab and washed out. If you're not sure which tones are right for you, hold several different sweaters or shirts next to your face and see which colors make your face look most alive. Another test is to stick with the colors you usually get compliments for wearing.

If you don't have that much faith in your judgment, read up on the subject. The idea of using color to enhance your appearance started some years ago with the publication of the paperback book *Color Me Beautiful* by Carole Jackson. It's still in print and should be available in your library or bookstore.

Any steps you take toward improving your appearance will be totally worthless if you're not into good grooming. Take a shower and change your socks and underwear every day. Make sure your hair is attractively cut, shampooed, brushed, and combed as often as needed. Wear clothes that are clean and fit right. Take good care of your teeth so you won't be ashamed of your smile.

Aside from that, there are only three other rules:

## *Looking Good*

1. Stop comparing yourself to TV stars and models who get paid to look spectacular.
2. Stop telling yourself you're ugly. You may start to believe it.
3. Stop worrying about your flaws. You'll never look good with a frown on your face.

# EIGHT

# When the Grown-ups Get to You

If your parents, stepparents, or teachers do things that hurt, anger, or embarrass you, you probably worry every time they do them. In between, you worry that they *might* do them, and on the side, you worry about how you can make them stop.

There are no easy answers to any of these worries, for the simple reason that you can't control other people's behavior. Your only hope—but it isn't a bad one—is to change the way you react to it.

## *Parents*

No matter how much you love your parents, you must know they're not perfect; but some are more imperfect than others. If yours drink too much or have violent arguments or feud with the neighbors, try to accept the fact that you're not responsible for their behavior. No matter how much it worries you, it's their problem, not yours.

There's an old saying, "You can't choose your relatives." It's a good thing to remember in these situations. It's also good to remember that your parents' problems don't reflect on you. Fair-minded people will judge you on your own merits, not on how the rest of your family behaves.

If one, or both, of your parents is determined to smoke, abuse alcohol or drugs, or take other types of risks, don't feel that it's your job to save them. It's unlikely that any amount of begging or pleading on your part will do it anyway. The decision to kick destructive habits has to be made by the people who have them.

While you can't tell your mom and dad how to behave, you can certainly tell them how their behavior affects you. Discussions of this type are never easy, but there are several things you can do to keep them from going off the track. Choose a quiet moment, don't resort to anger or self-pity, and be sure to keep the focus on you, not them— for example, "I really worry when you drive too fast" or "I have a hard time getting to sleep when you and Dad are arguing about money again."

Your comments may not result in any changes, but you'll feel better for having gotten the problem out in the open and making your feelings known. Taking some type of action is usually better than sitting still and letting things happen. If nothing else, it makes you feel less helpless.

There may be times when your parents upset you by not doing something you think they should. Perhaps you're unhappy with the appearance of your home, the community you live in, the school or church you attend, or how you spend your vacations. You may have a point, but whether you do or not, your parents are the ones who have the final say in such matters.

Instead of grumbling and fretting, it would be easier—and smarter—to put up with their decisions. When you get right down to it, you have no other choice.

Liz Claiborne always wanted to become a fashion designer, but her father was dead-set against the idea and insisted that she study art instead. Claiborne bowed to his wishes, but she took additional courses in pattern making and sewing on the side. When she finished school and was ready to go job hunting, she headed straight for Seventh Avenue—the center of New York's fashion industry.

As you get older, you may understand the reasons behind your parents' decisions. You may also find, as Claiborne did, that their ideas aren't totally off the wall. The designer has never been sorry she studied art. "It taught me color, proportion, and many other things that I don't think I would have learned in design school," she says.

## Divorce

If your parents' marriage is in the process of breaking up, you've got a lot of heavy-duty worries. One of them may be unraveling the mystery of what went wrong. Marriage is such a complex relationship that your mom and dad may not fully understand the situation themselves. The one thing you can be sure of, though, is that the breakup had nothing to do with you.

Your next worry may be that your friends will treat you differently because of the divorce. You can forget that one, too. Some of them have probably been through the experience themselves. If they haven't, they know kids who have. Divorce is so common these days that except for the parties involved, few people give it that much thought.

If your friends do start avoiding you, it's probably because they don't know what to say about the situation or they're not sure how you're taking it. You can help them by mentioning it as matter-of-factly as you can and by letting them know that you're still the same person you were before your parents decided to split up.

Still another of your worries may be how the divorce is going to affect your day-to-day life. Can your mom manage without your dad around, or vice versa? Who's going to fix the car or do the cooking? You may also be concerned about money. Is there going to be enough to go around, or will you have to move to a smaller house or give up your plans for going to college? Then there's the even thornier question of what will happen if the parent you live with becomes ill or dies.

The only way to get answers to these and some of the other questions that may be bothering you is to ask. Your parents must have a fairly clear idea of what's going to happen when the divorce becomes final, but it may not have occurred to them that you'd like to know.

Tell either or both of them that you're worried and ask

them to sit down and give you a clearer picture of how things will go. A session of this type should alleviate some of your worries. It will certainly dispel the worst one: being kept in the dark.

## *Stepparents*

If your mom or dad decides to remarry after a divorce or the death of your other parent, you're going to have to deal with a stepparent. For most kids, that's an instant worry. Although you may not have enjoyed living in a one-parent family, you probably liked having your mom's or dad's undivided attention. Now you'll have to share it.

The arrival of a stepparent may also result in changes in some of the routines you were used to and liked. Things are always different when somebody new joins the family. Just because things are different, however, doesn't mean they'll be worse. In fact, they could be a whole lot better.

Your mom or dad may be happier and more relaxed with a new marriage partner. The household may run more smoothly with two adults to share the responsibilities, and although you may have to relinquish your role as your parent's confidant and companion, you'll also be relieved of the burden of sharing his or her problems.

Even if you can appreciate the advantages of the remarriage, however, you'll still have to adjust to being a stepkid. If you like your stepparent, you'll be off to a good start, but if you're not crazy about him or her, don't assume that all is lost. It will take time—possibly as long as a year or more—for you to get used to each other.

Even if you're not overflowing with affection, you can still be polite and cooperative with your stepparent. If you want to keep things on an even keel, don't criticize or treat him or her as an outsider, and don't make unflattering comparisons to the parent he or she has replaced. Above all, don't say things like, "You're not my *real* father [or mother]. You can't tell me what to do."

It's possible, of course, that you don't want to keep things on an even keel. You may be angry about the marriage, jealous of the new person in your parent's life, and fearful that your own needs will get short shrift. Such emotions are understandable—and also quite common—but don't use them as an excuse for stirring up trouble.

Try to sort out your feelings in your own mind. Face up to what's bugging you and, if possible, talk it over with someone who can listen without being critical. One of your friends or a sympathetic adult are good possibilities, but your best bet may be your real parent. He or she is the person most likely to be concerned about your feelings. Your real parent may also welcome the opportunity to discuss the new marriage and assure you that your interests will not be neglected.

If you have concrete areas of disagreement with your stepparent, don't let them fester. Talk them over with him or her, but do it without making accusations, being sarcastic, or losing your temper. Simply explain what's bothering you and why. Your stepparent may be happy to hear your point of view. Being a newcomer to the scene, he or she can't be expected to know your attitudes and habits or to read your mind. Quite often, stepparents have no idea how such matters as chores, curfews, and discipline were handled in the past.

Generally speaking, it's not a good idea to bring your real parent into your negotiations with your stepparent. He or she will dislike being put in the position of taking sides and may not stick up for you anyway. If the problem is primarily between you and your stepparent, try to keep it that way. You have to learn to get along with each other and the best way to do it is to work out your problems on a one-to-one basis.

It's rare for a stepparent to be as cruel and horrible as they are in fairy tales. Most of them are kind, decent people who are trying to do their best. Why not give yours a chance? You already have one thing in common—loving your mom or dad. That should give you something to build on. Before long you may grow to love your stepparent, too.

## *Extra-Strength Worries*

If a parent or stepparent is genuinely cruel to you, possibly even physically or sexually abusive, talk to your other parent about the problem. If he or she can't help, talk to your school counselor or psychologist or to one of your teachers. Don't worry about betraying family secrets. Your own well-being is more important.

School counselors and teachers may not be able to intervene directly, but they can suggest sources of help or arrange a meeting with your parents to propose that family counseling is in order.

## *Teachers*

Your teachers are in a position of authority over you just like your parents. If they expect things to be done a certain way, you'll save yourself a lot of hassle by not trying to fight them.

It's inevitable that there will be certain teachers you don't particularly like or respect. There's no need to let them know how you feel. Be polite and pleasant, even if it kills you. You might also try getting to know the teachers you dislike a little better. You may find that they aren't so bad after all.

It's equally possible that one of your teachers doesn't particularly like you. Make sure you're not doing something—like being disruptive in class or failing to do your work—to cause it. If you plead innocent on both counts, why not try letting the teacher get to know *you* a little better? A gesture of friendliness on your part could make a difference. When you make the effort to be nice, even confirmed grouches will often respond by being nicer to you.

Although the grown-ups in your life may do any number of things that strike you as mean, rotten, thoughtless, or unfair, don't ever use their bad habits to justify your own. Maybe your father is too strict or your mother always favors your big sister or your homeroom teacher has put you on his blacklist. Irritating as their behavior may be, there's no point in getting back at them by being surly or disobedient or breaking every rule you can find. You won't be hurting them, you'll be creating more worries for yourself.

# NINE

## Friends and Foes

Of all the worries you have to put up with, the worst may be the ones that are inflicted on you by kids your own age. Even your closest pals may not always treat you as well as you'd like. Worse yet, you may be afraid to complain for fear of losing their friendship. But sulking in silence isn't a good idea either.

If one of your friends says or does something that hurts you, don't stalk off in a huff or sneak away to nurse your bruised feelings. Stand your ground and speak up. Tell him or her you didn't like it and ask if it was meant to hurt you.

You might also request some clarification, such as, "Did I hear what I think I heard?" or "Why did you do that?" Direct questions are a good way to defuse indirect hostility. Sneaky people hate to get caught.

Sometimes it's a good idea to look behind your friends' actions. They may have some hurts of their own to unload and you're a handy dumping ground. If you suspect this is the case, why not give them the benefit of the doubt?

If your own hurts aren't too serious, the simplest response may be to pass the whole thing off with a smile or a funny remark. Disagreeable people don't always realize what they're doing, but if they were being unpleasant on purpose, letting them know they haven't offended you may discourage them from trying again.

## Breaking Up Is Hard to Do

It's a toss-up which is worse: being dropped by your best friend or deciding to drop him or her instead. But friendship is a two-sided affair. If either one of you is dissatisfied with the relationship or feels you no longer have that much in common or has simply found a new best friend, a breakup is inevitable.

If you're the one who gets pushed aside, you may feel abandoned, hurt, angry, or perhaps all three. You're entitled, but there's no need to make a scene or tell off the other person. It won't do any good, and it could destroy your chances of resuming the friendship at a later date. Accept your fate as gracefully as you can and start paying more attention to your second-best friend.

If your former best friend was also your one and only, you'll be more worried about finding a replacement. Don't panic; look around. There may be a new kid in your class or someone who's also lost a friend. Or you may be able to team up with another pair of best friends and make it a threesome. As long as you don't try to gang up on, or squeeze out, one of the original twosome, it may work very nicely.

Another solution is to latch on to a larger crowd. You'll probably find a favorite in the group, but neither one of you will be totally dependent on the other for companionship.

The situation can be almost as worrisome when you're the one who wants to end the friendship. Try to do it with a minimum of hard feelings. Don't pick a fight, break a date, or unleash a barrage of scornful or insulting remarks. Ease your way out of the relationship by not calling up as often and being less available after school and on weekends. Your friend will soon get the message.

There will be some worries, and possibly some guilty feelings on your part, when your old best friend sees you with your new one. The encounter will also have the potential for snubs and slights, but don't be the one to initiate them. Smile and say hello and hope that your discarded buddy will be mature enough to do the same. Even though your best friend days are over, you don't have to become deadly enemies.

## *Your Popularity Rating*

Being popular is a common worry among kids. It's at the root of such other worries as not looking like Kirstie Alley or Tom Cruise, or not owning closets full of designer clothes or a state-of-the-art cassette player. In reality, looks and possessions have very little to do with the problem.

It's possible that you have an unrealistic idea of how many friends you need. You don't have to be the most sought-after kid in the class, and even though you yearn to belong to the In crowd, the world won't come to an end if you're not. Think in terms of quality, not quantity. As a wise man said, "If you have one true friend, you have more than your share."

If you're lacking even one friend, true or otherwise, it could be that you're new to the school or the neighborhood and it's going to take you a while to fit in. Another possibility is that there are certain aspects of your own behavior that turn people off. Perhaps you come across as snobby or standoffish when you're really just shy. Or people may think you're conceited because, in your desire to overcome your insecurities, you keep telling everyone how terrific you are.

It's equally possible that you've been targeted for teasing and exclusion through no fault of your own. Kids can be terribly mean to each other. They'll often pick on someone just for the fun of it. No matter how much it bothers you, try not to lose your cool. The whole point of the abuse is to make you miserable. If you pretend to be indifferent, you'll spoil the fun and sooner or later your torturers will give up.

When actress Darryl Hannah was in high school, the other kids teased her for being so tall and skinny and called her names like Toothpicks and Beanpole. Hannah found a way to make herself more popular. She put on funny outfits and sang silly songs in morning assemblies. Her talent won her the leading roles in several school musicals, and before long, the teasing stopped and she was accepted as one of the crowd.

If you're not up to performing in public, you should be able to find other ways to make friends. Capitalize on your talent for writing by submitting a story to the school paper. Sign up to sell ads for the yearbook. Offer to help with the cleanup after the class picnic.

They say that the best way to have a friend is to be one, so make an effort to reach out to other people. Be quick to smile and say hello or to strike up a conversation with one of your classmates. Find an excuse to call some of them up or invite them to a party. It may take time, but eventually you'll find someone you like who also likes you.

No matter where you go or what you do, you're always going to run into people who could make your life unpleasant if you let them. Don't let them. Assume they're doing the best they can and try to make allowances for their shortcomings. But don't ever blame yourself for their failings, and above all, don't spend any more time with them than you absolutely have to. Spend it with people who give you happiness, not grief.

# TEN

# Putting Worry to Work

When you're knee-deep in worry, you can always count on some cheerful soul to tell you, "There's no point in worrying," or, "Worrying doesn't do any good."

It's not only maddening, but like so many other things people tell you, it's not always true. When you let your worries prod you into solving your problems, worrying can do a surprising amount of good.

In 1990, singer Gloria Estefan's tour bus crashed on a snowy highway and she was rushed to the hospital with a broken back. The doctors repaired her fractured vertebrae, but a month after the accident she was still in pain and unable to walk.

The prospect of being confined to a wheelchair would be enough to frighten anyone, but it was an even bigger worry for Estefan. Her father had been in a wheelchair for many years, and she remembered what a trial it was for the whole family.

Determined to do everything possible to avoid such a fate, Estefan asked her doctors if they knew of any special treatments that might help her regain the use of her legs. They couldn't make any promises, the doctors told her, but her one hope was to embark on a long, tedious exercise and weight-lifting program.

Estefan gritted her teeth and did it. A year after her accident, she was not only back on her feet, she was twisting, leaping, and dancing her way through a two-hour show in Miami that was the first stop on a forty-one-city world concert tour.

Gloria Estefan licked a major problem because she knew how to put worry to work. You can do the same thing with many, if not all, of your worries. Basically, it's a matter of common sense, but since your common sense is apt to go flying out the window when you're worried, here's a quick review of the four basic steps:

1. Find out if the problem is solvable.
2. Figure out what's causing it.
3. Decide how to solve it.
4. Do it.

## Is the Problem Solvable?

Don't be too quick to dismiss a problem as hopeless. It may not be. Such things as your athletic ability and your brains are to some extent givens, but that's no reason to convert them into given-ups. Instead of telling yourself, "Nothing will help," or, "What's the use?"

see if there isn't something you can do to improve the situation.

If you made a serious effort to follow the phys ed teacher's instructions, you might not be the biggest klutz in gymnastics class. Some extra attention to your studies may not turn you into an A+ student, but it could cure your C sickness.

Many problems get relegated to the unsolvable file because the people who have them don't think it's their job to solve them. When something goes wrong, they blame it on fate, bad luck, or somebody else. The coach doesn't like them. The teacher is an airhead. The test was too hard. Another kid made them do it.

If you tend to look for scapegoats for your troubles, ask yourself if there's even a remote chance that you might be contributing to the problem. If the answer is yes, you can also contribute to the solution.

## What's Causing It?

You'll never solve any problem until you know what's causing it. To find out, you may have to explore several possibilities. Suppose you're on the verge of flunking math. It could be because math is your least favorite subject so you give it the least attention. It's also possible that you don't like the teacher and it shows—which means that you don't have much hope of getting extra help or special consideration. Still another explanation: You're operating on a shaky foundation because you haven't mastered the fundamentals.

Most problems lend themselves to this kind of analysis, but some people are too aggravated by their worries to try it. Others are reluctant to probe too deeply because they're afraid of what they might find. Deep down in their hearts, they may know that they're falling behind in their assignments because they're spending too much time on the phone or glued to the tube, or that they could get along better with their moms and dads if they did things the first time they were asked or, better still, didn't wait to be asked at all.

## How Can It Be Solved?

Causes usually lead to cures. In the case of the mortifying math grades, for instance, you may need to make math your first priority rather than your last, or adopt a more positive attitude toward your teacher; or maybe your best bet would be to find someone to tutor you in the basics so you won't feel so lost in class.

Some of the problems you encounter may have more than one solution. Be ready to try them all. If the one that seems best doesn't work, go on to the next one. When Georgia Governor Andrew Young, who has also served in Congress and as ambassador to the United Nations, was growing up in New Orleans, his father hired a professional boxer to teach him to fight. If any of the white kids in the neighborhood called him "nigger," Andy was instructed to talk first but be ready to slug it out if talking failed.

## *Do It*

Depending on the nature of your problem, finding a solution may be simpler than applying it. Most people resist change, especially if it's going to involve some work on their part. They'd rather put up with their worries than go to the trouble of solving them.

There's another whole group of people who think that worrying absolves them of the need to do anything else. A classic example is the person who's constantly forgetting to do things—and just as constantly apologizing for it—and yet never makes the slightest effort to keep track of what needs to be done.

There are also people who—perhaps without even realizing it—use their problems as a way of getting sympathy or attention or as an excuse for not doing well in other areas. If they solved their problems, they'd have to stop thinking of themselves as victims and start taking more responsibility for their lives.

If you're honestly worried about your problems, you should be willing to do whatever it takes to solve them. If you're not, you may have to break down and admit that you're not as worried as you claim to be.

If you have problems that don't lend themselves to any easy solutions, here are three suggestions that may help:

### 1. Make the most of what you've got

When the First Lady of the American stage, Helen Hayes, started out in the theater, she was told that although she had a great deal of talent, she wasn't tall enough to be a star. The five-foot-tall actress responded by becoming what she describes as "the tallest five-foot woman in the world." She did such a good job of making people forget her diminutive size that she was eventually cast in the role of Mary of Scotland, one of history's most statuesque queens.

California Angels pitcher Jim Abbott is an even more remarkable example of someone who overcame his liabilities by capitalizing on his assets. Abbott was born with only a single stump of a finger on his right hand and yet he managed to play quarterback for his high school football team, pitch for the University of Michigan baseball team, earn the 1987 Sullivan Award as the country's best amateur athlete, win the gold-medal baseball game in the 1988 Olympics, and get drafted to pitch for the Angels.

## 2. Turn minuses into pluses

Julius Rosenwald, the merchandising wizard who served as president of Sears, Roebuck and Company for many years, had a favorite saying: "When you have a lemon, make lemonade."

That's one way to turn a minus into a plus. The case of fourteen-year-old Jane Brown is another. When Jane's mother was transferred to the London office of her advertising agency, Jane found herself not only the new kid in the class, but a foreigner besides. Her English classmates made fun of her New York accent and taunted her for being a Yank.

Jane's mother thought of transferring her daughter to

another school or giving her speech lessons so she'd sound more English. Then she decided to follow one of the lessons she'd learned in advertising—when you have a good product with a slight drawback, you don't try to conceal the drawback, you play it up as something special.

Following her mom's advice, Jane stopped wearing her British tweeds and trying to blend in with the crowd, and returned to her New York uniform—a blue denim skirt and jacket and a T-shirt with a picture of a frog and KISS ME in six-inch letters. The other girls were fascinated, and in no time at all, *Yank* became a term of affection rather than derision and Jane became one of the most popular girls in the class.

## 3. Keep trying

If you can't solve your problems at the first crack, keep trying. Sometimes persistence is all it takes. An experimental psychologist named K. Raaheim has devised an innovative way to test human intelligence. It's called the Hat Rack Problem, and it consists of giving the subjects two poles, a clamp, and a hat and asking them to make a hat rack.

The most intriguing thing about this problem—which can be solved by securing the poles together with the clamp, wedging the result between the floor and the ceiling, and hanging the hat on the clamp—is that, of the hundreds of people who have tried it, about half usually get it right.

There's no way of predicting on the basis of education or background who they will be. The only conclusion Mr.

Raaheim has been able to draw from his research is that the subjects who ultimately succeed make more unsuccessful attempts.

When you make up your mind to put worry to work, you'll be tempted to go after your biggest problems first. They're the ones you most want to get rid of. Resist the temptation and start with the small ones. Think of them as warm-up exercises. They'll get you in shape for the more serious challenges.

Even if you become a grand master in the art of putting worry to work, you may still find yourself up against problems that are beyond your power to solve. Don't burden yourself with a new worry by deciding you've failed. There are some situations you just have to live with. It may be a discouraging prospect, but the good news is that even if you can't get the better of your worries, you can definitely keep them from getting the better of you.

## ELEVEN

# How to Live
# with Your Worries

"What can't be cured must be endured" is a rhyme you've probably heard a zillion times. It may be trite, but it's also true. There are two kinds of endurance, however. One simply holds on and hopes for the best. The other takes steps to ease the strain.

If you've got a worry that can't be solved, go for the second kind. Controlling your response to the problem, even if you can't control the problem itself, will make you feel less at the mercy of your worries and will also help you hang in while you're waiting for things to improve.

If you want to develop this kind of endurance, here are four rules to get you started:

### 1. Take care of yourself

Good things look bad and bad things look worse when you're not feeling your best, so the first step in your war against worry should be keeping yourself healthy. Get plenty of sleep. Eight hours is the recommended amount. You may need more, but don't try to survive on much less.

You should also be careful of your eating habits. Don't swear off meat or embark on any fad diets without consulting either a doctor or a trained nutritionist. You could be depriving yourself of essential vitamins and minerals. Skipping meals is a no-no, too. You can't deal with stress if your body is undernourished.

It goes without saying that you should steer clear of alcohol, drugs, and tobacco. Alcohol and marijuana are particular menaces because, aside from all their other drawbacks, the former is a depressant and the latter can make you feel panicky. It hardly makes sense to fool around with them when depression and anxiety are the very sensations you're trying to fend off.

## 2. Get plenty of exercise

According to one group of psychiatrists, worry is what your mind does when your body is feeling tense. If you can work off some of that tension through exercise, your mind will relax, too.

Not everyone is interested in, or good at, team sports, but there are other ways to keep active. Your community may have facilities for swimming, handball, tennis, or golf. Sports such as running, bicycling, roller-skating, and aerobic exercising don't require any special facilities.

One of the easiest, cheapest, and least time-consuming

ways to exercise is walking. Try doing a mile or two—more if you want—a couple of times a week.

You can exercise alone or with a friend, but be sure to do it regularly, not just when you're in the mood or have nothing better to do. A fitness routine will improve both your physical and your mental health and give you a better shot at keeping your worries under control.

### 3. Be good to yourself

People sometimes get the idea that bad things happen to them because they themselves are bad. They then proceed to punish themselves for their imaginary sins by forgoing some of the ordinary pleasures that everyone deserves.

The people who do this don't realize they're doing it, of course, but if you have a tendency to neglect your appearance, to feel guilty when you're not doing something useful, or to be kinder and more forgiving of other people than you are of yourself, you may be blaming—and punishing—yourself for your worries. There's no reason to. You're not responsible for problems that aren't of your making. So stop depriving yourself of experiences you might enjoy. It won't solve your worries. On the contrary, it will only make you more depressed.

### 4. Keep busy

Have you ever noticed that you tend to think about your problems when you're lying in bed at night, or sitting through a long-winded speech or boring movie? Whenever your mind is at rest, your worries take advantage of the lull and move in. The best way to keep them out is to have other things to think about.

In 1945, after leading Great Britain to victory in World War II, Prime Minister Winston Churchill was resoundingly defeated in his bid for reelection. Instead of brooding about his rejection by the voters, he spent his newly acquired free time writing his best-selling six-volume history, *The Second World War.*

Chinese pianist Liu Chi Kung managed to take his mind off an even worse set of worries. In 1958, Liu became a world-famous virtuoso after he placed second, behind Van Cliburn, in an international piano competition held in Moscow. A year later the young musician was declared an enemy of the Chinese state and thrown into prison for seven years. Liu made good use of those years. He spent the time rehearsing all the pieces he had ever played, note by note, in his head. Within months of his release, he was back on the concert stage and, as the music critics agreed, playing better than ever.

You should be able to find something to keep you from wallowing in worry and self-pity and possibly even add to your accomplishments in the bargain. Take up carpentry, cooking, or photography. Join the glee club. Try reading every book in the library. Become a volunteer at a local hospital, nursing home, or soup kitchen.

When you're busy and active, you won't have as much time to worry. In addition, your problems will seem less humongous because they'll be balanced against the other satisfactions in your life.

\*     \*     \*

Even if you follow these rules to the letter, you may not succeed in completely conquering your worries. If you have serious problems, they're sure to get to you now and then. Here are some steps you can take to reduce your anxieties when they do:

## 1. Talk it over

You may be reluctant to share your worries with anyone, but as Splinter, the wise old mouse, remarks in the movie *Teenage Mutant Ninja Turtles,* "The path from inner turmoil begins with a friendly ear."

If you've been keeping your problems to yourself, consider talking them over with someone. Another person may be able to give you some useful advice or help you develop a new perspective on the situation. If nothing else, you'll feel better for getting the problem out in the open.

Naturally, you'll want to confide in someone you trust. Your best friend is a logical choice, but if you have reason to doubt his or her discretion or loyalty, you'd better find someone else—your parents, perhaps (unless they're part of the problem), or a sympathetic relative, a favorite teacher, clergyman, or neighbor.

If you can't bring yourself to talk about your worries or can't find the right person to talk to, try putting them down on paper. Recording your worries in a diary will relieve you of any fear of embarrassment or punishment. In writing about your problems, however, don't simply present or rehash the facts. Describe your feelings about the situation. Giving vent to your hidden sorrow, frustration, or rage will relieve you of a substantial amount of inner stress.

If your worries are particularly burdensome, consider seeking professional help. Alcoholics Anonymous has special programs for the children of alcoholics. Planned Parenthood can advise you about sexual concerns. There are also any number of social services agencies, such as the Family Service Association, Jewish Family Service, and Catholic Charities, as well as community hotlines and youth counseling services that specialize in helping people in trouble. You should be able to find them in the yellow pages under SOCIAL AND HUMAN SERVICES.

## 2. Teach yourself to relax

When your mind is teeming with worries, the only thing to do is shut it down and clear them all out. You can do this by calling up a soothing image on your mental screen and concentrating on it to the exclusion of everything else.

Try focusing on some pleasing object—perhaps a room or a house you particularly like—and describing it to yourself in minute detail. If you're not particularly visual, inhale and exhale very slowly ten times and concentrate on your breath as it enters and leaves your body.

These are simplified versions of a technique called imaging, which is even more valuable in reducing anxiety. Imaging requires some—but not a whole lot of—practice. Start by finding a quiet spot and then sit or lie down and close your eyes. Imagine the most peaceful scene you can think of—a meadow, a mountain lake, the seashore, a kite drifting through the sky on a summer day. Now lose yourself in the scene. Think of the sights, sounds, and smells, the sunshine, the breeze, the sense of contentment you feel when you view it. If other thoughts enter your head, acknowledge them and then quickly discard them.

Keep the image in your mind for as long as you can. In the beginning, it may be only a minute or less, but if you work at it, your concentration time will gradually increase to five or ten minutes. That's all you should need to get out of your worry mode and into a calmer frame of mind.

## 3. Try prayer

In one form or another, prayer has helped millions of people all over the world achieve peace of mind. Even people who aren't particularly religious often find it a help in times of trouble. Your prayers don't have to be long or formal. Praying is just a conversation between you and God in which you place yourself in His hands, tell Him about your problems, and ask Him to help you live with them.

When United States Navy pilot Lieutenant Robert Wetzel was shot down over Iraq during the Persian Gulf War, he suffered two broken arms and a smashed collarbone. His captors saw to it that his injuries were treated, but as soon as he was well enough to leave the hospital, he was transferred to an Iraqi prison. He was locked in a cold, dark solitary cell, slapped around by

Iraqi guards, and forced to live on a once-a-day ration of broth and pita bread.

Still in pain from his injuries, Lieutenant Wetzel had no idea when, if ever, he would be released. He also had to live with the knowledge that he might be tortured or executed at any minute. Wetzel sustained himself with a combination of prayer and imaging.

He imagined himself walking down the streets of his hometown of Metuchen, New Jersey. As he came to each house, he stopped and said a prayer. Those prayers, says Wetzel, were the only thing that kept him going during his nerve-racking ordeal.

Although living with your worries is your only option at the moment, that may not always be the case. Some of the things that make you feel odd or different at this stage of your life may not matter so much later on. Problems that strike you as hopeless right now may lend themselves to solutions up the line. If there's trouble at home, you can take comfort in the knowledge that eventually you'll grow up and go out on your own.

James Michener had to live with two unsolvable problems when he was young. The first was that he was adopted and never knew the names of his natural parents. The second was that the widow who adopted him periodically ran out of money and had to send him to live at the local poorhouse.

Michener escaped the poverty of his childhood by working hard in school and winning a scholarship to college, but he never succeeded in tracking down his real parents and finally gave up trying. How does the author live with that worry? "I just don't think about it that much," he says.

Believe it or not, you, too, may reach the point where your most excruciating worries lose their sting. That doesn't necessarily mean you'll be worry-free. As your current worries subside, new ones may come along to take their place. But not to worry. If you learn to live with the ones you have now, you'll be able to live with those, too.

# TWELVE

## Winning against Worry

Yogi Berra once said, "Ninety percent of sports is mental. The other half is in your head." His percentages may not add up, but he's got the right idea. Attitude is as much a part of winning as training and talent.

Attitude is also a factor in how well you handle your worries. If you'd like to be able to take your troubles as they come, to resist falling apart under stress, and to feel challenged rather than discouraged by problems, you've got to develop the right attitudes.

### • Keep your eye on your objective

In the summer of 1986, a fourteen-year-old Japanese-American violinist named Midori was playing Leonard Bernstein's "Serenade" at Tanglewood, with the composer himself conducting the orchestra. Suddenly the E string on her violin snapped. The teenager turned to the orchestra's concertmaster, who handed her his own Stradivarius. She tucked it under her chin and coolly resumed her playing.

A few minutes later, the E string on the Stradivarius also snapped and Midori was forced to use the associate concertmaster's violin. In spite of the interruptions and the fact that both violins were considerably larger than the instrument she was used to, Midori completed her performance as flawlessly as if nothing unusual had happened.

At the conclusion of the piece, audience, orchestra, and composer-conductor Bernstein joined in a cheering, stomping, whistling ovation. It was a tribute not only to the young violinist's brilliance as a musician, but to her ability to remain unfazed by circumstances that would have rattled many a more seasoned performer.

Afterward, Midori confessed that she didn't understand what all the fuss was about. She had come to Tanglewood to play a violin solo, and that's what she had done.

If you want to avoid coming unglued when things go wrong, keep your eye on what you're trying to achieve and don't be deterred by the minor, although often distressing, problems that crop up along the way.

### • Be adventurous

If there's something you'd really like to do—take a trip, join a special class, participate in an unusual project—don't back off with lame excuses like "I've never done it before," or, "None of my friends are doing it," or, "I might not like it." Give it a try.

Every time you get involved in something that goes

beyond your usual routine, you're providing yourself with the opportunity to develop new skills, meet new people, and adapt to new situations. In the process, you'll develop something the mental health experts call *mastery*—the sense of security and self-confidence that comes from mastering challenges. The feeling will carry over into other areas of your life and you'll be less intimidated by unfamiliar situations and problems. Instead you can tell yourself, "I handled that. I can handle this, too."

Being adventurous can also offer other rewards. During his college days, Muppets creator Jim Henson had a part-time job as a puppeteer on a Washington, D.C., television station. He loved the position, but he never saw it as a serious career possibility. "It didn't seem to be the sort of thing a grown man works at for a living," was the way he explained it to an interviewer.

After thinking it over for a while, Henson decided to do what he enjoyed. His decision led to the creation of the Muppets, which not only became a multimillion-dollar property, but brought fun and laughter to children and adults all over the world.

• **Take charge of your life**

Some experts claim that kids worry more than grown-ups because they have less control over their lives. In many ways that's true, but don't let that keep you from taking charge of the areas in which you do have some control.

There's an old adage, "To get along, go along." It's good advice in some situations, but if you follow it in others you may get involved in things you don't like or shouldn't do, or in trying to be someone you're not. Instead of going along with the crowd on everything, be selective. Do only what's right for you.

Cleaning up your room and organizing your closet and dresser drawers may not be your idea of a good time, but bringing order out of chaos is another way to gain a sense of control. So is managing your time. There's a close relationship between hurry and worry, aside from the fact that they rhyme.

If you want to avoid the feeling of being trapped in a never-ending game of beat the clock, don't leave things until the last minute. Be aware of how long it takes to do them and allow yourself enough time, maybe even a little extra just to be on the safe side. If there are chores you dislike, such as setting the table or doing the dishes, performing them in slow motion will only prolong the agony. Do them and get them over with so you'll have that much more time for yourself.

The more you take charge of the various aspects of your life, the more competent you'll feel. And feeling competent is often the first step in *being* competent.

• **Live in the present**

You may have enjoyed the zany time travel that made *Back to the Future* such an entertaining movie, but don't try to duplicate the stunt in your own life. There's nothing to be gained from harkening back to the past or pinning all your hopes on the future. Maybe you were happier in your old neighborhood or your former school. Maybe you'll be happier when you learn to drive or find a steady girlfriend or boyfriend, but why let that stop you from making the most of the here and now?

Shirley Temple Black, the former child movie star who had a second career as a United States ambassador, tells a story she heard from her husband, Charles. As a boy, he asked his mother what her happiest moment had been.

"Right now," was her reply.

"But what about the day you were married?" Charles demanded.

"My happiest moment *then* was *then*," she told him. "You can only live fully the moment you're in. So to me that's always the happiest moment."

It can be yours, too, if you put aside your memories of yesterday and your dreams of tomorrow and live for the one day that's within your grasp—today.

### • Believe in yourself

The New York Giants went into the 1991 Superbowl with what most sports fans thought was a serious handicap. The Giants' regular quarterback, Phil Simms, had been sidelined with a foot injury and their only choice was to use an inexperienced backup, Jeff Hostetler.

Not even Hostetler's teammates expected him to come through. In the locker room at halftime, he had to put up with cracks like, "You're just a backup," "You can't win," and "When's the last time a backup quarterback won a Superbowl?"

Hostetler ignored them all. He believed that he could win the game for the Giants, and he did.

If you want to stay comfortably ahead of your worries,

you've got to believe in yourself. That doesn't mean being self-centered and conceited. It's important to know your limitations, but don't underestimate your strengths.

You may not be a star athlete or the class brain, and your looks may be only so-so, but you can find plenty of other reasons to feel good about yourself. Perhaps you can sing or play the guitar. Maybe you're handy with tools or quick at figures. You may have a knack for cheering people up and making them smile. Your abilities don't have to be earthshaking, but no matter how modest they are, be proud of them and proud of yourself for having them.

If you can develop these attitudes—and there's no reason why you can't—you'll find that you don't have as many worries as you used to and that those you do have are easier to tolerate. You won't be immune to problems—nobody is—but no matter what happens, you'll never be so paralyzed by worry that you can't fight back.

# Index

# Index

YA

152.46   Fleming, Alice
FLE         Mulcahey, 1928-

What, me worry?

$12.95  18/28/92

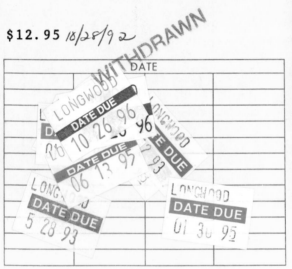
LONGWOOD PUBLIC LIBRARY

BAKER & TAYLOR BOOKS